HOPSCOTCH

"Sausages!"

First published in 2002 by
Franklin Watts
96 Leonard Street
London
EC2A 4XD

Franklin Watts Australia
56 O'Riordan Street
Alexandria
NSW 2015

Text © Anne Adeney 2002
Illustration © Roger Fereday 2002

A CIP catalogue record for this book is available
from the British Library.

ISBN 0 7496 4700 0 (hbk)
ISBN 0 7496 4707 8 (pbk)

Series Editor: Jackie Hamley
Series Advisor: Dr Barrie Wade
Cover Design: Jason Anscomb
Design: Peter Scoulding

Printed in Hong Kong

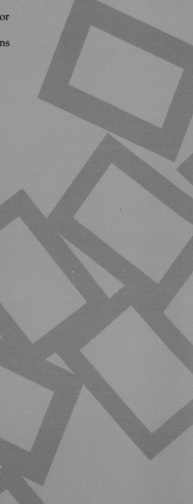

"Sausages!"

by Anne Adeney and Roger Fereday

W
FRANKLIN WATTS
LONDON•SYDNEY

Once there was a poor man called
Albert who needed some new shoes.

Albert asked the village shoemaker
to make him some fine, new shoes.

But when they were ready, he
couldn't pay for them.

"It's clear that you don't have enough money to pay for these shoes," said the shoemaker.

"But I know how you can pay and it won't cost you a penny," he added, with a smile.

"How?" asked Albert.

"From now on you must only say one word, 'Sausages!'" the shoemaker told him.

"You mustn't say anything else
until we meet again!"

"Sausages!" agreed Albert and he
hurried home.

"You're late," grumbled Albert's wife. "What have you been doing?"

"Sausages!" replied Albert.

"What did you say?" she
asked, crossly.

"Sausages! Sausages!" Albert
shouted, trying not to laugh.

Albert's wife was worried. She rushed next door to ask her neighbour for help.

"Come quickly!" she yelled.

"There's something wrong

with Albert!"

The neighbour hurried next door.

"What's wrong, Albert?" she asked.

"Can I get you anything?"

"Sausages!" came the reply.

"He's lost his mind!" wailed
Albert's wife.

"I'll fetch the mayor," promised
the neighbour. "He might help!"

The mayor came to visit Albert.

"What's the problem?" he asked.

"Sausages!" replied Albert.

"What?" shouted the mayor.

"Sausages!" Albert said again,

feeling very silly.

Soon the whole village knew that there was something wrong with Albert and he could only speak nonsense. Albert was embarrassed.

The next day, the mayor visited
the shoemaker.

"Have you heard the news?" asked
the mayor. "Albert has gone mad!"
"Rubbish!" replied the shoemaker.

24

"He has!" said the mayor, crossly.
"He only says 'Sausages!' when you
talk to him! He makes no sense!"

So the shoemaker played his little trick. "I bet you fifty gold coins that Albert is not mad," he said, knowing the mayor was rich.

"It's a deal," agreed the mayor,

and they went to find Albert.

"Hello, Albert!" said the shoemaker.
"Sausages! – oh, I am pleased to see
you!" answered Albert. "Now I don't
need to say 'Sausages!' any more.

The whole village thinks I'm mad

because of this sausage talk. These

shoes have certainly cost me a lot!"

"Not as much as they've cost the mayor!" the shoemaker laughed, as the mayor handed him fifty gold coins.

So the shoemaker was paid for his shoes after all. Now Albert pays his bills on time. And the mayor has never made a bet again!

Hopscotch has been specially designed to fit the requirements of the National Literacy Strategy. It offers real books by top authors and illustrators for children developing their reading skills.

There are 12 Hopscotch stories to choose from: